Unity in Diversity

Ukiyoto Publishing

All global publishing rights are held by

Ukiyoto Publishing

Published in 2024

Content Copyright © Ukiyoto

ISBN 9789364948005

All rights reserved.
No part of this publication may be reproduced, transmitted, or stored in a retrieval system, in any form by any means, electronic, mechanical, photocopying, recording or otherwise, without the prior permission of the publisher.

The moral rights of the author have been asserted.

This is a work of fiction. Names, characters, businesses, places, events, locales, and incidents are either the products of the author's imagination or used in a fictitious manner. Any resemblance to actual persons, living or dead, or actual events is purely coincidental.

This book is sold subject to the condition that it shall not by way of trade or otherwise, be lent, resold, hired out or otherwise circulated, without the publisher's prior consent, in any form of binding or cover other than that in which it is published.

www.ukiyoto.com

Contents

Divided yet United!	1
By Kajari Guha	
Poems By Rhodesia	10
Struggle for freedom verses struggle for oppression: The Berlin Wall	18
By Aurobindo Ghosh	
Short Stories By Dr.Yogesh A Gupta	37
The Tree of Harmony: A tale of Unity in Diversity	51
By Moumita De	
In Memory of a Great Flood	57
By Dr. Renuka KP	
About the Authors	*69*

Divided yet United!

By Kajari Guha

A typical Monday it was. The rushing footsteps, the hurried greetings, the coffee cups crinkling and the keyboards clicking! Men and women dressed in uniforms settled at their desks, diving into emails preparing for the week that was peeping into the days ahead. The strategy sessions were planned. The meeting rooms were booked for the upcoming projects. The managers convened with their teams and set priorities. It was the start of the work week with a blend of lively conversations and focused concentration. ND Media House resounded with action. However, in the shadowed corners of the Media house, dirty politics thrived, undermining the actual morale and efficiency rooted in the organization.

At lunchtime, Mr.Anand, the Chief Editor,called Rishabh Deshpande and asked him if he could come over to his office.

Rishabh had completed his MBA and had got an offer from this big company as a trainee. As a newcomer, he enjoyed the thrill of starting a new chapter and the opportunities for growth and improvement. On the other hand, he felt uneasy due to the unfamiliar environment, sarcasm and subtle forms of ragging. When he was informed to report to the boss, he had butterflies in his stomach. He tried to get a self -appraisal. Yes! He had completed the Excel sheets quite well, yet he was apprehensive as he had been still learning about it. However, his stress got released when he found that it was only about the grapevine discussion. He was asked if he knew anything about the misinformation and the rumors. It was the need of the hour for the company to be transparent with its employees. So, he must be watchful about the gossips going on in the office and should inform his boss. Rishabh felt a bit relieved and answered what he knew, but all these reminded him of the monotonous cacophony of the survival of the fittest. He was a simple person who believed in the principles of 'unity in diversity'and not in the theory of 'divide and rule.'

"Let's break this monopoly of the monotone!" his heart echoed.

"How?" he asked secretly to himself.

"Take a leave for a few days and enjoy in the Nature's lap." murmured his heart, "but getting a job is not a child's play. How could I go on leave before I have done with my probation period? I am no more a kid and I have a number of responsibilities on my shoulder. My father is suffering from cancer. My mother is a housewife, and the old age has become a curse for her, physically and mentally. Everyday she is worried about her husband's health. I have a younger brother too who is still doing his studies. If I leave my job, all of them would be starving."

He kept on pondering over these issues when the phone rang, and he had to attend the call.

When he came out from the boss's cabin, his colleagues stared at him as if he had got a promotion. Some whispered to their friends,

"There is something fishy going on. Why did the boss call this newbie?"

"I guess it's about the Event that would be showcased next month." said Reshmi from Kolkata.

"Naaah dude! Nothing of that sort. He seems to be his relative, might be planning something special." said Bharti, from Orissa.

"Yaaahh…maybe you're right. I just hate this lout! He is from Maharashtra and would always cheer up his own state. He would always blame those who are from other states like Tamil Nadu, AndhraPradesh, Bengal, Bihar or Assam etc.as if Marathis can only fulfill the targets." interrupted Rashika from Delhi.

Monica from Arunachal Pradesh was smiling and was silently enjoying their conversation.

"Shhhhh——his watchdogs are coming. Get yourselves ready with the latest report." Soumya from Bihar muttered.

Soham and Sahil, the two managers were in a jolly mood, talking constantly about the upcoming Event that was going to take place in Delhi.

"Do you know the Prime Minister is going to be there this time?" Soham said.

"Nooowaayyy! You're not joking, are you? Now gird up your loins Soham. If you prove your mettle by hook or by crook, you're gonna rule over this Media House. You can teach a lesson to that lousy old man sitting in the cabin, smoking his precious British cigar all the time and manipulating each and every project and getting all the credit." Sahil retorted dramatically.

"God!!!! You really emphasized on that cigar huh!!! That's actually the best way to reign, you see." said Soham.

"'Power corrupts, and absolute power corrupts absolutely.' Our boss is the best example of that, but Sahil is the right hand of the boss. Why is he speaking against him?" Soham thought.

"I need to be careful talking to him. One day he might use me as his scapegoat, and I would land up in trouble.

"Here, the key decisions get influenced more by personal agendas than by the company's best interests. This toxic environment can bring ultimate disaster and decline in creativity and productivity." he thought, but he didn't have the guts to share it with anyone. He hurriedly moved towards his cabin. He wrapped up his pending tasks as the clock approached the designated hour of dismissal.

It was the end of the day that brought a noticeable shift in the atmosphere. Everyone organized his or her desk, shut down the computer, gathered the personal belongings and headed towards the exit. A few lingered for brief social interactions or maybe last-minute collaborations. Others made a beeline for the door. Oh! What a relief from the day's stress!Rishabh was about to leave, but Sahil called him to say that their boss had asked him to stay back for some urgent reasons. Rishabh felt a piercing pain in his chest, took a pain killer and waited for the meeting. Sahil and Soham were already there in the boss's cabin. He texted his younger brother that he would be late, and he must take care of Papa, should give him the medicines and ask mom to not worry about him. He would be home around eleven p.m as he didn't know the exact time when the meeting was going to start and end. It hadn't started yet.

After one hour of waiting, he was called in the boss's office.

Sahil and Soham were already there, doing something on their laptops.

"Hello young man!" The boss started, "Tomorrow, you have to leave for Delhi with Sahil for the event we are going to present. All the world-known presses are going to arrive. Day after tomorrow they would hold a meeting and you must get a know-how to do the presentation."

Rishabh was awestruck.It was just like his promotion. It seemed he had been able to win the boss's confidence and was in his good books. But what would happen to his father's chemotherapy? It was scheduled on the same day, and he had to be present in the hospital. He was in a dilly-dally, but he was unable to say anything. However, he was reminded of the quote,

"If the boss sings your praise, beware of his tricks as there is a little gap between the pat on the back and the kick on the pants." He smiled at his own joke. The meeting had come to an end after a few discussions. Rishabh left for home.

Next morning the day started as usual. It was the transition from personal freedom to professional responsibilities. Rishabh got too busy with the fresh bundle of files. He attended a meeting called by Sahil.They had to leave for Delhi in the evening. They discussed about the issues that could be raised and how to resolve them. They went to meet the boss to find out if anything else came up to his mind.

When they entered the office of their boss, Rishabh smelt something burning. However, he ignored. They were discussing on the project. Sahil asked Rishabh to present the important topics to be dealt on.Mr. Anand was smoking his cigar, the blue smoke going upward like the warmth emanated from the fireplace.

Suddenly there was a loud explosion and alarms blared loudly. Chaos and panic ensued as the smell of smoke began to permeate the air. Everyone jolted from his or her tasks grabbing the personal belongings. It was a transformation from an orderly office to a scene of frantic struggle. Everyone aimed to reach safety measures. Fire wardens were called who were trained for such emergencies. They directed the flow of the office-staff. There was a lot of hustle bustle. It was ensured by the wardens that evacuation routes were clear, and everyone could exit the building swiftly and safely. None was allowed to use the lift.

Rishabh and Sahil came out of the office and were completely shocked.Mr. Anand was still reluctant and was enjoying his cigar. Soham struggled through the crowd of the coworkers. Most of them huddled together. He entered the office and was stunned to see the carefree appearance of his boss, looking upward at the ceiling as if everything would be managed by the employees and the workers. He couldn't even make out that the fire was caused by the short circuit of a frayed wire in his cabin. There were sparks. Small flames were visible from the frayed wire. There was the smell of burning plastic and the sight of smoke alerted all, except the haughty, pot-bellied boss. The rapid response of fire safety systems and emergency services was crucial. The fire had to be controlled and it had to be prevented from spreading further. The smell of burning plastic and sight of smoke alerted all. They triggered alarms and evacuation procedures started. Some grabbed the fire extinguishers to attempt containment. Others ensured that everyone headed to the nearest exits.

"Sir! Please leave your seat and come out of your room." shouted Soham.

Reshmi, Rashika, Bharti and Soumya came running towards the boss's cabin.

"Sir! Please hurry up and be fast. The fire is spreading." They screamed.

Mr. Anand was in a fix. He reluctantly left his revolving chair, it seemed someone would grab his position if he left that seat. Then leisurely he took the cigar and his bag and was about to move towards the door when a plastic wire got ablaze and fell near the door. He headed towards the door. With his bulky belly it was impossible for him to walk towards the door of his office so that he could get out of the room.

Soham and Rashika rushed at him. The wire was ablaze, the flames dancing around like a belly dancer. The red and orangish fire was like a vindictive hyena looking for its prey.Mr. Anand was on the right-hand side of the door and the fire was in the left side. If he could hurry, he would be saved by God's grace from the wrath of the Fire-God.But he remained at the same place near his chair, not knowing what to do. It was not a sensational piece of news that could be bought with money, and he just couldn't find any solution.

Even if Rashika had been criticizing her boss so much just the other day, she forgot everything and rushed inside the room with Soham. Both of them extended their hands to Mr. Anand and pulled him together. Rashika took hold of the bag, and Soham supported him to come out of the room.Reshmi, Bharti and

Soumya had been waiting for them. Sahil and Rishabh also had joined them. Everyone was trying to get out of the building. The staircases were crowded with the hustle bustle of the employees. Managers, Executives, sweepers, peons… …all were equally disturbed and etched with concern. The fatality of the incident made them unintentionally united to meet challenges. They felt relieved after seeing their boss safe, having escaped the immediate danger. All the employees belonged to not only different caste and creed, but to various states and communities also, yet unitedly they stood together to fight against the impending danger.

When the whole building got evacuated, Mr. Anand thanked all his employees and colleagues.

"I don't have words to express how much grateful I am to all my colleagues who have saved me risking their own lives. I am proud of you all that you believed in the saying "United we stand, divided we fall." Love you guys." he said.

The tickets of Rishabh and Sahil for visiting Delhi were postponed. All of them headed home.

The ND Media House itself became a major sensation and their office got shifted to a nearby building.

Diamond Painting

Each person is a precious stone,
Crafted and carefully placed
By a master artisan
In a specific coordinate
Of space and time…

Some stones sparkle,
While others lack luster,
Each with its unique hue,
A signature vibration
It can proudly call its own…

No single stone is less prized;
For every one, regardless
Of luster, color, or size,
Is absolutely necessary
To complete a masterpiece…

A grand tapestry,
A diamond artistry,
Entitled "*Humanity*",
A composite of every man
In the history of mankind.

When East Meets West

How can the dawn meet the dusk,
Or the east be with the west?
Just one peep, is it too much to ask,
For their rendezvous to be set?

Why amidst all the freedom
Bestowed on the heavens above,
The earth remains imprisoned
Within its dogmatic rock?

While their union is pure magic -
An amalgamation of cultures,
Its un-fruition is so tragic,
Depriving possible futures.

A future of a better breed,
Humanity at its finest,
The day the heavens and earth kissed,
The golden moment east joins west.

Seven

Like an exquisite gift from seven heavens,
Are the colors traversing the sky in unison,
Tightly-knit, complete, and inseparable,
Seven distinct energies comprising a whole,
All the more varied, all the more beautiful.

If only the seven continents of earth
Can mirror the rapport in the rainbow,
Each area a distinct and significant part,
Every culture emitting its unique glow,
All the more diverse, all the more wonderful.

Coexisting peacefully, thriving equally,
Where the growth of one is the growth of all,
And the pain of one permeates the whole,
Where differences are not shamed but celebrated,
All the more distinct, all the more unified.

Symphony

How vibrant - this blue planet, from afar,
Pulsating life in every corner,
Like a symphony -
Of waterfalls, waves, and winds,
With the flutter of butterfly wings,
Flapping feet of penguins,
Morning chorus, mourning wails,
Silence and serenade.
Baby's first scream, first fill of air,
Voices, conversations, muffled messages,
Love, laughter, lullabies,
Sweet hellos and sad goodbyes.

Drifting dreamily in space,
Dancing on its own heartbeat
Of human emotions and experiences,
Scattered like fireflies on its surface,
A different tone, a disparate timbre,
A wavering tempo, a varying cadence,

A multitude of languages,
All trying to express and exchange,
To learn, to understand; to grow, to expand
The prevailing consciousness of man,
For only in embracing this diversity,
The earth can realize a harmonious unity.

Worldwide Web

We are all of us intricately linked
In a web of social ecosystem,
Perpetually maintaining a balance
For human society sustenance.

Each person, clan, and nation,
With a purpose and function,
Entirely its own -
A signature contribution.

From tomatoes to salmon,
From microchips to petroleum,
From nurses and caregivers,
To techies and teachers.

From prairies to mountains,
From deserts to oceans,
From rural to urban,
From virgin to modern.

We are all of us in one worldwide web,
And each vibration is transmitted
In a social neural link interconnected,
Where we are once and for all united.

Struggle for freedom verses struggle for oppression: The Berlin Wall

By Aurobindo Ghosh

Disclaimer:

1. Historically recorded facts and true incidences are not fictions.

2. This document contains relevant information collected through extensive research without addition or deletion.

3. Whether against the Dictatorship or Colonial regime, all those who fought are freedom fighters.

4. Popular names of freedom fighters are known to all and so the author tried to find some unsung heroes who sacrificed their lives for the same cause but never recognised.

5. The author is grateful to all who documented the sacrifices of many unknown freedom fighters through books, News papers, cinemas etc.

Limitation:

1. The Author has tried to summarize the story of

Hitler's Germany during World War II, without alteration of any incident recorded by historians. The author wishes to confess that as he does not know German language, he could not read or understand the meaning of famous speeches of Hitler and other German leaders.

Chapter 1
Backgrounder of Annihilation

Mahatma Gandhi, Indira Gandhi, Rajeev Gandhi of India, Sheikh Muzibur Rahman of Bangladesh, Julfikar Ali Bhutto, Benazir Bhutto, Zia-Ul-Haq of Pakistan, Nelson Mandela of South Africa, Abraham Lincoln, John F Kennedy, Martin Luther King Jr. of the USA, Adolf Hitler of Germany, Benito Mussolini of Italy, Saddam Husain of Iraq, Osama Bin Laden of Al Qaida and many others from different parts of this world, died of unnatural death either for their good work or for their bad work. Self proclaimed judges of the society, punish both good people and the bad people. They decide sitting in the dark room, when and how the social activist Martin Luther King Jr. or the preacher of non-violence Mahatma Gandhi would be eliminated. In other dark room, some other group plan to eliminate Mussolini, Hitler or Zia. Advocates and operators of both freedom as well as oppression are omnipresent everywhere on this earth. It will be a blunder to believe that all people of this world desire peace and harmony. There are many souls who enjoy instability and precariousness. We can call this situational fact as 'Hatred coexistence'.

Since last one and half century, world witnessed the bloodbath in African continent. Leaders one by one faced mysterious elimination systematically carried out with unknown reasons. Notable among them were Malcolm X, Martin Luther King Jr., Medgar Evers, Fred Hampton, Marcus Garvey, Patrice Lumumba, Steve Biko, Amilcar Cabral, Thomas Sankara, Walter Rodney, Chris Hany, Edgar Medici, Hector Pieterson, Rosa Luxemburg and Nita Barrow and many others.

Root cause of oppression:

The monarchies of Europe played a pivotal role in the establishment of expansionist traditions resulting colonialism as early as from 15th century onwards. This era marked by the age of exploration, also saw European powers extending their reach across the globe including Indian subcontinent, driven by a combination of economic interest, religious zeal and geopolitical ambition. The roots of European expansion can be traced back of the consolidation of powerful monarchies in countries such as Spain, Portugal, Austria, England, France and Netherlands. These monarchies, driven by a desire for enormous wealth and resources, embarked on overseas exploration to find new trade routes and territories. The long Christian campaign to recapture Spain and Portugal is known as the reconquista, meaning reconquest. Traditionally, the reconquista is said to have begun in 718, in the battle of Covadonga. In this battle Christians from the small kingdom of Austrias, in northern Spain, own a victory over Moors. This battle of recapturing process is perhaps the longest battle in the history of mankind. It completed in 1492. Acquisition of free resources and fervor for further conquest and exploration epitomized by the voyages of Christopher Columbus under the catholic Monarchs Ferdinand and Isabella.

Chapter 2

Causes of upsurge of intercontinental expansionism:

Monarchies played a crucial role in funding and legitimizing these expeditions. For instance, Prince Henry, the Navigator of Portugal spearheaded the early exploratory efforts along the West African coast, laying the groundwork for the Portuguese Empire. The Spanish Crown supported numerous expeditions to the America, leading to the conquest of vast territories. The treaty of Tordesillas (1494), brokered by the Catholic Church, divided the newly discovered lands outside Europe between Portugal and Spain, demonstrating the central role of Monarchies and religion in early colonial endeavors.

Economic motive was the offshoot of religious aggression on far away land. The primary economic motive of colonialism was the search for new trade route (such as silk route) and resources. Some primary and precious commodities like Silk thread, spices, gold, silver, emerald and other minerals were in great demand. The mercantilist economic policies of that era, which emphasized accumulating wealth through trade surplus and the exploitation of colonies, spurred European monarchies to establish and expand their overseas empires. Some of the empires which ruled most of this world are Portuguese empire, Yuan Dynasty, Umayyad Caliphate, Abbasid Caliphate, Second French Empire, Spanish Empire, Qing

Dynasty, Russian Empire, Mongol Empire, British Empire and Ottoman Empire or the Turkish Empire. Influx of enormous wealth in the respective treasury transformed those empires into pre-eminent global power.

Religious zeal also played a significant role in European colonialism. The spread of Christianity was often used to justify the subjugation and conversion of indigenous populations. Missions and missionaries accompanied the explorers and settlers, aiming to convert non-Christian populations and integrate them into the colonial system. Converted Christians were always rewarded with both money and kind. They were acknowledged as superior to non-converted locals. Innocent locals would be attracted to the superior standard of living of converted Christians and would get converted making the process a cyclical chain.

Chapter 3

Competition, Conflict and Impact on colonial regions:

Inevitable happened. As European powers expanded their territories, conflict of interest took its toll. Initially, the conflicts between states were minimal but as the bounty of loot became massive, the conflict grew lethal resulting war between them. The famous among them were the Anglo-Spanish war, the Dutch-Portuguese war and numerous Franco-British colonial conflicts resulting intense rivalry between European powers. The colonial population faced different types of problems when the power shifted to other party. For example, suppose a colony was administered by French Monarch for nearly half a century. The colonial people adapted the French culture as taught by the French bosses. All of a sudden British troop entered in the same territory. War began and British Monarch won the battle and the colonial alignment got shifted to British Monarch. From then onwards, the lives of locals now jeopardized. British culture and French culture collided to gain supremacy. After two three decades of British rule, the people started adapting the British culture including the language. In the same house the elders would follow French culture and the new generation would follow British culture. The impact of war was devastating. Both the French and the British were waging war against each other on a foreign soil. The indigenous populations were subjected to brutal conquest, forced labor and diseases to which they had no immunity. The demography of the region was subject to change. This culminated to transatlantic slave trade, driven by demand. This is the reason today we see millions of African families in all parts of Europe and America. These wars of expansionism resulted in reshaping the demography of entire world. Ultimately, the time arrived when the indigenous population understood the actual intention of the colonial Monarchs and started to think about their own independence. Slowly and steadily, they gained people's support to stage wars against the colonial ruler. One by one the countries became independent though the colonial influence had already changed the life style influenced by the prolonged governance of foreign states. Populations of many African countries, speak either Spanish or French or English as their national language. They have forgotten their own African dialect long back. They could not save their own identity. Recently a group of social scientists are engaged in unearthing these languages to save them from extinction.

Example:

Even after gaining independence the cultural beliefs remained as a life style. In India, after 75 years of independence, still majority of Indians feel that Britishers are the superior race and speaking English is a matter of pride. Even lower middle class Indians prefer English medium schools for their children.

How pathetic! In many homes, conversing in English is matter of habit. Many a times they are ashamed to talk in their mother tongue. Goa, a state in western part of India was under Portuguese rule, Pondicherry (Puducherry) in southern part of India was under French rule, a part of Bengal was under Dutch rule and rest of India was under British rule. Several regions of the world witnessed colonization by multiple countries and had been a recurring theme. Southeast Asia, the Caribbean, African subcontinent were under the colonial rule of multiple countries. Vietnam, Laos, Cambodia were controlled by French and Japanese. Indonesia was known as French Indonesia until WW II. After that Japanese took over its control. Most striking occupational changes happened in St. Lucia a Caribbean island, changed hands fourteen times between French and British between the 17th and the 19th century.

Chapter 4

Intra-state conflict in Germany:

In the previous chapters, we discussed about the inception of colonial rules by stronger nations on morally weaker nations. Even if they had natural wealth in abundance, they could not gather the necessary united strength to confront the aggressor. Even India could not realize the intention of the British merchant 'East India Company' who had come to invade and convert this vast nation into a colony. It happened to all other countries too.

One of the most influential European countries who too took part in expansion mechanism was Germany. This country faced many ups and downs. Once a thriving super power, Germany was made to kneel down on its own ground. It is a story of riches to rugs and then again bouncing back to its original format. It's a story of insanity, brutality, devastation on one side, determination, gallantry, courage and spirited minds on other side.

Historical facts:

After the World War I, and aftermath of the Treaty of Versailles, that imposed harsh penalties and reparations on Germany resulted in economic hardship and national humiliation. The situation was so worse that to remain alive having two square meals became a dream for majority of German population. They needed a leader very badly and urgently who will steer their ship from stormy water to a comparatively calm one. They saw that leader in Adolf Hitler. They needed an association to help them to cruise through the troubled economic hardship. National Socialist German Worker's Party (Nazi Party) was formed. Initially, Hitler did wonderful jobs to coordinate the different political groups to come together and motivated them to fight against the stringent economic sanctions imposed on them. He was a fierce orator and could mesmerize the whole lot of people whoever came to listen to his speeches. Slowly, he took Germany out of all economic, social, cultural and political problems. But at this juncture he slowly and steadily converted once popular Nazi party to an autocratic one. By the time general people could understand what was happening, Adolf Hitter had become the sole and powerful Dictator of Germany. He developed a vision for himself, and that was 'Germans are Aryan Master race'. Within a very short time he made Germany a powerful European nation. He could never forget the past humiliation of his country by other European nations. He always wanted to take revenge. At the same time Hitler developed an urge of exploring expansion of German territory like other European countries. His first aggressive invasion of Poland on September 1, 1939 triggered the Second World War which lasted six years and one day. It ended with the Japanese surrender on 2nd September 1945. Over 50 million soldiers and civilians lost their lives during this period. Hitler then launched offensive in the west on 10th May, 1940. Within a month, in June 1940, France surrendered to Germany. Just after two weeks, Germany attacked Britain on 10th of July 1940. The full fledged war known as The Battle of Britain began on 25th July 1940. The Blitz War (Lightening War) started on 29th December 1940. London was bombed on the night of 24 August 1940. The following night the British Prime Minister Sir Winston Churchill ordered an attack on Berlin, the capital of Germany. World saw more than one massive ruthless attacks like Russian invasion, Pearl Harbor, Nagasaki, Hiroshima and ultimately Japanese surrender.

Chapter 5

Hitler's Germany: A brief analysis of pre and post World War II:

As told earlier, in 1933, Hitler was appointed Chancellor of Germany. The name of the parliament building was Reichstag. On 27th February, 1933, one Mr. Van Der Lubbe set the Reichstag building on fire. He was immediately arrested. Using this incidence as a pretext Hitler passed the infamous 'Reichstag Fire Decree' suspending civil liberties. The Enabling Act of 1933 gave Hitler dictatorial power, allowing him to dismantle democratic institutions and suppress oppositions.

He swiftly implemented policies based on the ideology of Aryan supremacy and Anti Semitism (Against Jews). Jews, political opponents and other minorities faced persecution. In 1935 Hitler passed the most indiscriminating law of political history of all times, 'The Nuremberg Laws 1935' which stripped Jews of citizenship and rights. Hitler's foreign policy aimed at two important decisions; (a) Undoing the treaty of Versailles and (b) Expanding German territory. After remilitarizing Rhineland in 1936, he annexed Austria (Anschluss, 1938) and Sudetenland from Czechoslovakia leading to Munich agreement in 1938.

World War II and Germany's fate:

World War II began on September 1, 1939, when Germany invaded Poland. Britain and France declared war on Germany two days later. Germany quickly employed its Blitzkrieg (Lightening) tactics, using rapid and coordinated strikes to overrun much of Europe including France in 1940. The war expanded as Germany invaded the Soviet Union (Operation Barbarossa, 1941) and the Axis power formed, including Italy and Japan. The Holocaust, one of history's gravest atrocities, saw the systematic genocide of six million Jews and millions of others including Roma, disabled individuals and political dissidents in specially built concentration and extermination camps.

From 1939 to 1942, Germany fought war on several fronts. Greed to occupy foreign lands compelled Adolf Hitler to employ hundreds of thousands of his elite soldiers to a war which had no future but inviting doom's day. By the mid of 1942, the tide began to turn against Germany with significant defeats at Stalingrad and El Alamein. The Allies forces including the US, Britain and Soviet Union together launched successful offensive in North Africa, Italy and Normandy (D-Day, 1944). Allies forces by 1945, closed in on Germany from both east and west. Huge number of soldiers and civilians lost their lives. Allied forces started intensive search for the Master of crime Adolf Hitler. They failed to find him. Like a coward, he committed suicide in a bunker on April 30, 1945.

A week later, Germany surrendered on May 7, 1945. Hitler was not there to witness the ruined Germany broken and shattered. He did not have courage to take responsibility of his misdeeds and face trial. What a shame!!

Germany was divided into four occupation zones controlled by the US, Britain, France and the Soviet Union. The division eventually led to the establishment of two separate states in 1949: the Federal Republic of Germany (West Germany) and German Democratic Republic (East Germany). Before the post war reconstruction, the Nuremberg trial began to punish the war criminals in 1946.

Chapter 6

The infamous Berlin wall:

The Berlin wall stood as one of the most powerful symbol of the Cold war, representing the division between the communist east and the capitalist west. Its history is a testament of the political and ideological struggles of the twentieth century. Erected in 1961, the Berlin wall not only separated East and West Berlin but also became a tangible manifestation of the iron curtain that Winston Churchill famously described. Throughout the 1960s the contrast between the two German states became stark. West Germany experienced rapid economic recovery and growth, often referred to as the 'Wirtschaftswunder' or economic miracle, while East Germany struggled under a communist regime characterized by economic hardship and political repression. This disparity led to a mass exodus of East Germans seeking better opportunities in the west. By 1961, approximately 3.5 million people had fled East Germany, creating a significant brain drain and labor shortage in the East.

To halt this migration, East German government, with Soviet backing, erected the Berlin wall on August 13, 1961. Initially composed of Barbed wire and make shift barriers, the boundary was soon replaced with more formidable structure: a concrete wall 12 feet high and 27 miles long, fortified with guard towers, anti-vehicle trenches and a 'death strip' that contained tripwires and other deterrents. This barrier effectively sealed off West Berlin from the surrounding East Germany and East Berlin.

The Berlin wall not only physically divided the city but also symbolized the border division of Europe. Many East German tried to cross and got killed and few were successful in crossing the border. The wall on the western side acted as canvas for political expressions: walls were covered with graffiti and art that condemned the division and called for freedom and unity. But the eastern side was a story of control and sufferings.

After long 28 years of numerous agitation, protests, marches, economic struggles within the eastern block, the East German government allowed its citizens to free travel between East and West Berlin making the existence of the wall redundant. It was the beginning of the end of Cold war. On November 9, 1989 the great wall of division fell. Many innocent lives were lost to get back the long due freedom of the East Germany people. Today, remnants of the Berlin wall serve as a poignant reminder of the brutal past. Memorials and Museums dedicated to its history educate new generations about the consequences of oppressive attitude, and the value of freedom and unity. The Berlin wall's legacy endures as a powerful symbol of resilience and the underlying human spirit in the face of oppression.

Epilogue

In the heart of Berlin, a wall did rise,
Dividing the city, splitting the skies.
Brick upon brick, cold war and austere,
A symbol of division of sorrow and fear.

On the East and the West, lives torn apart,
Families sundered hearts heavy and smart.
Graffiti and Barbed wire, stark and tall,
Stories of struggle etched in the wall.

Yet hope persisted, as whispers grew loud,
Voices of freedom breaking the shroud.
Till one fateful night, the wall gave way,
To dreams and reunions, to a brighter day.

Now a relic of history, a lesson to all,
Of unity's power of division's fall.
Berlin stands free, a testament clear,
That wall of oppression can disappear.

Short Stories By Dr.Yogesh A Gupta

We are different, We are the same

India is a country whose preamble declares it to be a sovereign, socialist, secular, democratic, and republic nation. It upholds the principles of equality, liberty, fraternity, and justice for all. However, since 1947, we have witnessed the divisive tactics inherited from the colonial rulers. They employed a divide-and-rule strategy to maintain their power, and even as they departed, they left behind the lingering wound of Hindu-Muslim conflict. The pain and humiliation of the 1947 partition remain unforgettable for both India and Pakistan. Over time, some wounds have healed, and India has evolved into a diverse nation, experiencing exponential growth and development across various sections of society.

Despite this progress, the advent of the digital age and increasingly toxic politics have given rise to a fabricated sense of division within society. However, those who live and work among different communities can attest to the true unity and diversity that exists. During festivals, medical crises, or environmental disasters, people come together to help each other, irrespective of caste, creed, or religion. Governments, regardless of their political affiliations, engage in welfare activities without discrimination. Unfortunately, the media often portrays a different, more hateful picture.

As a doctor, I witness what many do not. I see unity in diversity and love all around. I firmly believe that the true character of a society or country is revealed in times of crisis or personal hardship.

I work in a multi-specialty hospital where over 50 specialty doctors tirelessly serve patients. Our nephrology department, in particular, has made significant strides over the past decade and is considered one of the best renal transplant departments. Patients from Gujarat, Rajasthan, and Madhya Pradesh come here with hopes of receiving better treatment for kidney issues. Thousands come for dialysis, and hundreds await kidney transplants. Many hope for an organ donation from a brain-dead patient, while others have loved ones willing to donate an organ to save their lives.

One such person was Rafiq Khan, a small-time businessman from Rajasthan. He lived a peaceful and content life with his wife Suhana and their two children, Ayesha and Athiya. His parents lived in a nearby house with his younger brother and his family. In the neighborhood, they were considered an ideal family, enjoying life and thanking God for His support and guidance.

However, not all days are good. God tests people with hardships as well. During a malaria epidemic in the state, Rafiq contracted a severe case of the disease. Though he recovered, the illness had permanently damaged his kidneys. His condition worsened, progressing from medication to needing dialysis. Like many patients seeking better treatment, Rafiq came to Ahmedabad. Since my hospital is the oldest in the city, many patients are familiar with it by name. Rafiq's family brought him to the nephrology department, and his treatment began.

For a year, Rafiq underwent dialysis every 15 days. Eventually, the senior nephrologist advised a kidney transplant. The news was devastating for the family, as Rafiq was the sole breadwinner, the children were too young, and his parents were elderly. But in trying times, relationships are tested. Suhana decided to donate her kidney to Rafiq. That day, the whole family cried and questioned why they were facing such trials despite their faithfulness, charity, and the good values they taught their children.

Suhana, however, strengthened their resolve by saying, "Rafiq, don't curse God. He has given the disease, but He has also provided the treatment. He has given me the strength to make this decision for the better future of our family and children. We will get through this together and emerge stronger with God's help and guidance."

The next day, they returned to the hospital and informed the doctors of their decision. As doctors, we are not surprised by such acts of selflessness because we witness them daily. Such acts reinforce our belief in God and motivate us to treat every patient with dedication.

Suhana underwent all the necessary tests to determine if her kidney was a match. A day passed with all the testing, and the results were a shock to everyone: her kidney was not a match. As doctors, we are always prepared for such outcomes, especially in married couples where blood groups often differ. Once again, Rafiq and his family faced despair.

Rafiq and Suhana had been coming to this hospital for a year. Every 15 days, they came for dialysis and, over time, became familiar with many other patients in similar situations. Suffering together often leads to friendships, and they got to know a lot about each other's families, jobs, children, and past lives.

One such patient was Prabhu Sharma, a schoolteacher from Madhya Pradesh. He was a middle-aged man with a wife, Seema, a child named Suraj, and his mother living with him. Prabhu had been suffering from knee pain for a year due to chikungunya, which he contracted the previous year. The constant pain and his job, which required him to stand all day, led him to consume a lot of painkillers. One day, while taking these painkillers, he suffered from severe diarrhea and vomiting, which led to dehydration. Due to inadequate medical care, Prabhu developed kidney issues.

Initially, the doctor was hopeful that his kidneys would recover since the damage was due to dehydration. However, the prolonged use of painkillers had already caused significant damage. By the end of three months, Prabhu and Seema were informed that he had chronic kidney disease, meaning permanent damage, and he would require dialysis. The family was in disbelief and sought opinions from several doctors, but each time their hopes were dashed as the diagnosis remained the same. Eventually, they accepted the reality.

Relatives advised them to seek treatment in Mumbai or Ahmedabad, known hubs for kidney disease treatment. Seema had many friends in Ahmedabad, so they came to my hospital and enrolled in the Nephrology department. After a few months of dialysis, the doctor advised a kidney transplant as the best solution. Prabhu had no suitable donor and feared he would die waiting for a kidney from a brain-dead patient.

Seema loved Prabhu deeply and knew she had to be the one to donate her kidney. She expressed her willingness to Prabhu, who initially refused, not wanting to jeopardize her health. He argued that one of them needed to stay healthy for their child. However, Seema consulted the doctor, who explained that one kidney is sufficient to live a healthy life, and this way, they could both support their child. After much persuasion and with a heavy heart, Prabhu agreed. But, as fate would have it, Seema's kidney was not a match for Prabhu.

Seema and Suhana had become best friends over the past year. While their husbands underwent dialysis for hours, the two women spent their time talking. They became like sisters, and their children started calling them so. A particularly emotional moment occurred when Suhana tied a Rakhi to Prabhu, and Seema did the same to Rafiq. Throughout this challenging year, the children enjoyed all the festivals together. It was heartwarming to see the kids studying the Geeta and the Qur'an with the help of their respective mothers. Suraj greeted Ayesha and Athiya with "Salam Alaikum," and Ayesha and Athiya responded with "Jai Shree Ram." People in the dialysis room drew strength from their example, believing that even a fraction of their positive attitude could help them through their own difficult times.

When both families received the news of the mismatched kidneys, Seema and Suhana cried for each other. Seema, being educated, started researching every aspect of organ donation, government initiatives, and enrollment programs. She discussed her findings with Suhana, and they sought information from every possible source. Although they were middle-class families with children to support, they had self-respect and did not beg for money. Instead, they applied for loans and government schemes to secure the necessary funds.

One day, while reading, Seema came across the concept of a SWAP kidney transplant, a legal method for families with mismatched donors who could match with other families. Seema saw a glimmer of hope and discussed it with Suhana.

Suhana asked, "Seema, what is this SWAP transplant?"

Seema explained, "Suppose Rafiq needs a kidney, and yours is not a match. Prabhu also needs a kidney, and mine is not a match. If your kidney matches Prabhu and my kidney matches Rafiq, we can do a kidney transplant. This is called SWAP, meaning exchange or crisscross."

Hearing this, Suhana jumped from her seat and exclaimed, "Ya Allah, thank you! If this is possible, then we sisters can have a happy life together."

She eagerly added, "Seema, come on, let's go and talk to the doctor. Let's do it right away."

Both were very happy. They went to the doctor and inquired about the SWAP transplant. The doctor was surprised to hear this, as she was unaware of their close friendship. She explained everything about the SWAP transplant and the legal protocols involved.

Both families readily gave their consent. As if God's test was over and the results were out, the matches were perfect. All government protocols were completed, and with due approval and consent, the kidney transplants for both patients were successfully performed.

A year later, both families live as neighbors in Madhya Pradesh, as Rafiq moved there. They live like close-knit relatives, and all three children are learning the valuable lesson of unity in diversity.

Unity Amidst Chaos

V.S. Hospital, a government institution nestled in the heart of Ahmedabad, Gujarat, was unusually quiet on the morning of January 26th. Despite the national holiday, Dr. Aman, Dr. Mehul, and Dr. Somesh found themselves on emergency duty, their faces etched with frustration as they trudged through the hospital wards, tending to patients and handling dressings.

"Happy Republic Day, huh?" Dr. Mehul muttered sarcastically as they made their rounds.

"Yeah, tell me about it," Dr. Somesh grumbled. "We should be home, relaxing."

Just then, a piercing cry shattered the air. "Doctor, please help me! I'm feeling severely dizzy," Ashma, a patient, called out, her voice trembling with fear. Dr. Aman, who had been feeling slightly lightheaded himself, rushed to her side. As more patients began to voice similar complaints, his suspicion grew.

"Something's not right," Dr. Aman said, his voice edged with concern. Suddenly, the ground beneath them trembled violently. The hospital building shook, and chaos erupted. People screamed and ran in all directions, some shouting that it was an attack by a neighboring country.

"It's an earthquake!" Dr. Mehul shouted, his face pale. "We need to get out of here!"

As they scrambled towards the ground floor, the doctors realized the gravity of the situation. At the second floor, cries for help from the ICU and surgical wards reached their ears. Dr. Aman, Dr. Mehul, and Dr. Somesh exchanged determined glances and raced towards the ICU.

The scene in the ICU was dire. Ten patients on ventilators were gasping for air, the power cut off by the earthquake. Relatives stood helplessly by, their faces masks of panic.

"Dr. Mubin, Dr. Bhavin, Dr. Gaurav, over here!" Dr. Aman called as more medical personnel arrived. Nurses Shamina, Ritika, and Irshan joined them, their faces set with resolve.

"Listen up," Dr. Aman said, addressing the relatives. "We need your help to pump air into the patients using Ambu Bags. We'll show you how."

Together, they worked methodically, teaching the relatives to use the manual resuscitators. The doctors and nurses moved swiftly, dividing tasks and stabilizing patients.

"We need to evacuate them to a safer place," Dr. Somesh urged. "Let's call the ward boys for assistance."

With the help of ward boys and additional staff, they began transferring patients to a more secure location.

Despite the chaos, their coordinated efforts brought a semblance of order to the situation.

As they finally reached the ground floor, the scene was one of utter devastation. People cried out for help, anger and fear mingling in the air. Amidst the suffering and confusion, a remarkable sight unfolded. Healthcare workers of all religions, citizens from every walk of life, came together, driven by a common purpose.

"We've got to keep going," Dr. Mehul said, his voice firm. "These people need us."

For days after the earthquake, this unity in diversity shone brightly. Healthcare workers, regardless of their backgrounds, worked tirelessly, day and night, to aid the survivors. In the face of overwhelming tragedy, their collective strength and compassion became a beacon of hope for all.

In the aftermath of the disaster, V.S. Hospital stood as a testament to the indomitable spirit of humanity, where unity triumphed over chaos and suffering.

Echoes of Unity: A Story of the Ram Temple

Anil, an Indian architect, stood proudly before the majestic Ram Temple in Ayodhya. He had been eagerly awaiting the arrival of his old friend, James, a historian from England. James had always been fascinated by India's rich history and cultural tapestry, and Anil knew that this visit would be special.

As James arrived, his eyes widened at the sight of the temple, its pristine white Makrana marble gleaming under the sunlight. "Anil, this is incredible," he said, awe evident in his voice. "The architecture is breathtaking."

"Wait until you hear the story behind it," Anil replied with a smile. "This temple is a living testament to India's unity in diversity."

James listened intently as Anil began to narrate the tale. "India has a long history of unity in diversity, James. Despite numerous attempts to divide us, from Mughal rulers to British colonizers, and now even some social media misfits, India stands strong. The Ramayana, one of our ancient epics, is a perfect example of this unity. It tells the story of a king, Ram, who united with tribals, Adivasis, a monkey king, and common men to defeat the demon king, Ravana."

As they walked towards the temple entrance, Anil pointed to the different materials used in its construction. "This temple is a symbol of that same unity. The core is made of Makrana marble from Rajasthan, while Karnataka's Charmundi sandstone with its exquisite carvings takes center stage. The entrance gate's figures are carved from pink sandstone from Bansi Paharpur, also in Rajasthan."

James marveled at the intricate details. "It's like each stone and carving tells its own story."

"Exactly," Anil agreed. "And it goes beyond just the materials. Gujarat contributed a 2100 kg Ashtadhatu bell that will echo through these halls, along with a 700 kg chariot carrying a special 'nagada'. The black stone for Lord Ram's idol comes from Karnataka, and the intricately carved wooden doors and handcrafted fabrics from Arunachal Pradesh and Tripura add to the temple's grandeur. Brassware from Uttar Pradesh and polished teakwood from Maharashtra also play a significant role."

They reached the temple's main hall, where the Ashtadhatu bell hung majestically. Anil continued, "On the day of the Pran Pratistha, or consecration ceremony, India witnessed an unparalleled display of unity in diversity. Over 150 saints from various traditions and 50 major personalities representing tribal traditions participated. People from all social hierarchies were involved as Yajmanas, or ritual performers."

James raised an eyebrow. "I've heard criticisms about India's caste system and discrimination. How did this event address that?"

Anil smiled. "During the ceremony, individuals from all walks of life, including Doms, who are caretakers of cremation grounds, Vanvaasi (tribal) people, Valmiki community leaders, nomadic community leaders, and members of the Lingayat community, performed the rituals. For the first time in our history, people from forests, hills, coastal areas, and islands came together to participate in a single event. It was a profound display of unity."

James nodded, clearly impressed. "This is remarkable, Anil. It's a powerful message to the world, especially in these times of division and misinformation."

Anil looked out at the temple, a sense of pride swelling in his chest. "India has always been more than what some might try to portray. Lord Ram's life was about uniting people, and his birthplace has once again proven that unity. Despite the challenges, our roots in unity run deep."

As they stood there, absorbing the atmosphere, James turned to Anil. "Thank you for sharing this with me. It's an experience I'll never forget."

Anil nodded. "I'm glad you could be here to witness it. This temple is more than just a structure; it's a testament to our enduring spirit of unity in diversity."

In the heart of Ayodhya, the Ram Temple stood not just as a monument of faith, but as a beacon of unity, shining brightly in a world often divided.

The Tree of Harmony: A tale of Unity in Diversity

Short Story By Moumita De

Long ago in Panna, a peaceful village of Madhya Pradesh, nestled between the rolling hills of Vindhya range and lush green meadows, there stands an ancient banyan tree known as the tree of Harmony. This tree was not like any other, it had vibrant leaves of every color imaginable, and each leaf represented a different story, culture and tradition from around the world. Hailing from the villagers believed that the tree of Harmony was a symbol of their unity in diversity.

Every year, the village celebrated a grand festival of colors. During this festival, people from various backgrounds, cultures and traditions came together to celebrate their differences and commonalities. The village was a mosaic of cultures, with families hailing from far-off lands, each bringing their unique customs, foods and stories.

One bright and sunny morning, preparations for the festival of colors were in full swing. The air was filled with the aroma of delicious foods from different parts of the world and the sound of laughter and music echoed through the village streets. The village children with their eyes wide with excitement, eagerly helped their parents decorate the village square with colorful ribbons, lanterns and flowers.

Amidst the preparations, a young girl named Mili, stood gazing at the Tree of Harmony. Mili was known for her insatiable curiosity and her love of stories. She often wondered how the tree came to be so magical and why it was so important to the village. Her grandmother, a wise and gentle lady, noticed Mili's fascination and decided to share the story of the Tree of Harmony.

"Come Mili", her grandmother said, guiding her to a cozy spot under the tree. "Let me tell you a story about how this tree came to be".

Long ago before the village was founded, the land was inhabited by different tribes. These tribes were often in conflict, each believing their way of life was superior. The land was plagued by discord and the people suffered as a result. One day, a wanderer named Amani arrived in the land. Amani was a wise and kind soul, who had traveled far and wide, learning about different cultures and traditions. She carried with her a mysterious seed, which she claimed had the power to bring peace and harmony to the land.

Amani gathered the leaders of the tribes and told them about her vision. She explained that the seed she carried could grow into a magnificent tree, but it needed the love and cooperation of all the tribes to thrive skeptical but hopeful, the leaders agreed to put aside their differences and work together to plant the seed she carried could grow into a magnificent tree, but it needed the love and cooperation of all the tribes to thrive. Skeptical but hopeful, the leaders agreed to put aside their differences and work together to plant the seed.

Each tribe contributed something unique to the planting of the seed. One tribe brought fertile soil from their homeland, another provided crystal clear water from a sacred spring and yet another sang an ancient song of growth and renewal. As they worked together, they began to understand and appreciate each other's customs and traditions.

With the combined efforts and unity of the tribes, the seed sprouted and grew into a beautiful tree with leaves of every color. The Tree of Harmony stood as a testament to what could be achieved when people embraced their differences and worked together towards a common goal. Over time, the tribes merged to form a single, diverse community, which eventually became the village we know today.

Mili listened intently, her eyes sparkling with wonder. "Grandmother is that why we celebrate the festival of colors? To remember the importance of unity in diversity?"

"Yes, my dear, her grandmother replied with a smile, "the festival reminds us that our differences make us stronger and more vibrant, just like the leaves of this tree. It's a celebration of the beauty that comes from diversity and the strength that comes from unity".

As the sun began to set, the village square was transformed into a kaleidoscope of colors. Lanterns of every hue illuminated the night, and the villagers gathered around the tree of harmony to begin the festivities. There were tables laden with exotic dishes and the air was filled with the tantalizing scents of spices, sweets and freshly baked bread.

However, the celebration took a dramatic turn when a fierce storm suddenly rolled in. Dark clouds gathered overhead and the wind howled through the village. The villagers, who had been singing and dancing moments before, now huddled together in fear.

The tree of harmony, which had stood tall and proud for generations, began to sway dangerously in the wind. Its colorful leaves were ripped away, scattering like confetti in the storm. The villagers gasped in horror as a massive lightning bolt struck the tree, splitting its trunk with a deafening crack.

Mili, clutching her grandmother's hand, felt tears stream down her face, "grandmother, the tree! What will happen to our village now?"

Her grandmother's eyes were filled with determination, "We must remember the spirit of unity that brought us together. We can save the tree if we stand united."

Hearing her determined words, despite the raging storm, the villagers rallied together. They formed a human chain around the tree of harmony, shielding it from the wind with their bodies. The tribal elders chanted ancient incantations, calling upon the spirits of their ancestors for protection.

Slowly the storm began to subside. The winds calmed, and the rain softened to a gentle drizzle. The villagers, soaked and exhausted, watched in awe as the tree of Harmony began to heal. The split trunk mended itself, and new leaves sprouted, more vibrant and colorful than before.

The Tree of Harmony stood as a testament to the villagers' unity and resilience. The storm had tested their strength, but their bond was unbreakable. As dawn broke, the village was bathed in a golden light and the Tree of Harmony shimmered with renewed vigor.

Mili looked up at the tree, her heart swelling with pride. She realized that the true magic of the tree was not just in its colorful leaves, but in the unity and love that it inspired among the villagers.

The festival of colors continued, now with a renewed sense of purpose. The villagers danced and sang, their hearts full of joy and gratitude. They promised to always cherish their diversity, to always celebrate the unique beauty f each individual leaf on the Tree of Harmony.

And so, the village thrived, a beacon of unity in diversity, a place where every story, every culture and every tradition were valued and celebrated. The Tree of Harmony stood as a symbol of their collective strength and the boundless possibilities that arose when they embraced their differences and worked together as one.

The end.

In Memory of a Great Flood

Short Story By Dr. Renuka KP

"Hohoihoi save me, save me" Parvati, widow of an ex-serviceman, shouted from the terrace of her two-story mansion. She made such a voice when she saw a fishing boat moving through the water where the land and sea were seen as one due to the terrible flood.

But the boatmen did not pay attention. The fact is that they did not hear her voice in the sound of rain. The boat was rushing to save some children stuck in a nearby college without food or water for two days. Parvati's screams were drowned out by the sound of the pouring rain and the roar of the wind. she started waiting there anxiously again hungry. what a crisis this is. She wondered how she would survive this. Will she sit frozen to death here? Fear began to haunt her. She was worried and did not know what to do. Then she sat on a chair near the wall and covered herself with wool.

It is raining heavily outside. Heavy wind was blowing from time to time and blowing the rainwater on the terrace. Then she was moving accordingly. Sitting there she looked around. Many tapioca and banana plants were all broken and fell with the wind. The branches of the mango tree and jackfruit trees were seen broken. The coconut trees were rotating in a circle in the wind. What if it falls on the top of the house? No one to help. Even if anyone came to know What else can they do? Her body began to tremble at the thought.

Parvathi came to the top of the house without any other solution to escape from this flood that entered the ground floor of her home. The Meteorological Center had informed that there would be no shortage of rain immediately. Everyone near her house went to rescue shelters. Parvati moved to the upper floor while all the other families moved to safer places. That was her fault. Those who moved to safe places got enough food and clothes along with the protection of the community. But Parvati was left alone. It has started raining continuously for three days. Aren't all the dams opened? A situation that has not been seen in Parvati's life till now. Heavy rain, wind and flood. Parvathy's house is located in a relatively high area. When there was a small flood, the water would not enter there. So she was watching the news on TV without much worry. Everyone is seen as so much afraid. What an excitement was to the reporters at the beginning of the flood.

Every channel shows high excitement when they get sensational news as the excitement and happiness of the Purakkatu coastal residents when they get a good chakara ie., a lot of fish suddenly, and claims that it is to them that this news first gets. What crazy they are to get sensational news.!

Forgetting all the political conflicts, the central government has given the support of the army itself for help. Where is the politics, where is the humanity? Since the heavy rains, the National Disaster Management Force has already also come down. All the roads had become a river within this time.

In any case, it is good that all the children are abroad. Otherwise, they may also have to suffer all these disasters. Now staying there They are watching the news on TV and giving their mother necessary guidance from time to time. Both of Parvati's children are studying abroad. It was heard saying by Old people the story of floods in the year sixty-one and ninety-nine in the past. Mother had said that Parvati wasn't born at that time.

'The flood in Ninety-nine, the elder of Paru,janu's breastfeeding time. Taking that small child we escaped to the Sree Moolam club by sailing in our small boat. There was a boat in the house that day. It was the father who rowed the boat through the rushing water. It was a life-threatening journey. My God, I had heard about the flood in 1961, but I had to experience it, my God.' she had heard frequently said her mother like this.

Yesterday, when everyone left their home, she should have gone too. but she thought she was safe on the upper floor. Her family is wealthy in that area. Moreover, she had collected some emergency things for this period of flood. Little did she know that a terrible flood was coming. Knowing that she was alone, the relief force came and called her.

'Paruamme, come with us. The water will not go away suddenly here, aren't the dams open?'

'Sorry, I may stay in the upper part ' she said humbly. hearing this their boat moved fast to the next destination. The woman next door also had called her,

'Sister come with us, the water is still rising. The rain is continuously pouring down.'

Even then, she did not think about escaping and going with them ..Perhaps although her life was in danger in the flood, they might have thought that the caste and religious thoughts by her birth had not left her so far. Remembering, Parvathy felt very sad.

It is a disaster caused by the stupid administration. All the dams overflowing above storage capacity were opened urgently to prevent them from bursting. How many Lives were washed away in that water? So many dreams and so many desires were abruptly destroyed. How many people became orphans? Who is responsible for this? Many survivors have no place to rest their heads to regain their lives. They lost everything they had earned until then and lost valuable things. It's just that somehow got life back.

Her house is a little higher in those areas. Since she got the warning, she has kept the food and some necessary items at the top as per her daughter's advice. She put the stove and firewood there. But on the first day, she started to be afraid of loneliness. Now she can hear only the sounds of people passing by searching for life. The first day she found comfort by calling the relatives and talking to them. But no one can reach her because everyone had already left seeking their safety.

'What a stupid thing you did!'

'Why don't you go to the camp?' somebody asked her.

'It was a mistake, I thought the water would not rise this much', she replied.

The point is true. The flood did not stop as Parvati expected. The ground floor was flooded in a single day. There was no broadcast on the TV in the evening. The electricity connections were also damaged in the wind. She did not even know that a family was swept away by the flood in the eastern region. All the low-lying areas turned into an ocean. Now the public has taken up the relief work.

That's when the fishermen arrived like angels. It seems that some felt wise at the last moment. The fishermen with their fishing boats helped many people in this crisis. All able people including the entire youth joined in the rescue operation There are a lot of small canoes and boats in the water floating for relief work. There is no caste, no religion, no politics, just trying to save human life anywhere. In the meantime, people are giving helpline numbers on radio and TV to help to move to a safe place.

She looks around with fear and sees a cow floating away. There are many living things floating in the water.. She can not see well due to the heavy rain. There are also many boats and canoes around to save them. It may be a last-ditch effort to save all.

Parvati stood up from there and looked down by getting on the staircase. All the newspapers and decorative items in the showcase have been washed away. Some dirty waste things are clinging there. Then she found a small creature on the top of the cupboard. She got scared. She came down to the balcony and shouted. No one was there outside to hear her voice. She went in fear to an upper room.

'Oh God, please stop this rain,' she prayed inwardly. Then she heard a voice and looked out of the window.Meanwhile, her phone was also turned off.

Parvati shouted when she saw a boat going.

'Come and save me 'she shouted. But they did not listen. Then she went to the terrace again and sat there . Now she can see only the roofs of the buildings and some creatures clinging to them. Trees are swaying in the occasional rain and wind When she heard a sad voice, "Bey Bey", she saw a baby goat sitting on the stump of a tree. She felt sad when she saw it. Pets and wild animals were floating around in the water. Oh my God, what a rain it is , she sighed.

Parvati has been sitting on the top of the terrace seeking help since yesterday. Fishing boats are now a lifesaver in places where even the army and the government have stopped. The roaring sea, sea-swept shores,, the crashing waves, the swaying boats, etc had already become their best friends while they trying to make their lives both ends meet. What is there that they cannot do? When Brittas, a fisherman, said that a woman who did not know the value of life tried to pay him while saving her life, many people bowed their heads. Some people are trying to save their pets rather than human life. What kind of views! The entire building of the biggest rich man there was open to the locals was a good flood scene

Incessant rain and wind. All the dams have overflowed. One of the old dams always spreads fear during the rainy season. Those who live in downstream are always living in fear of seeing the dawn. Journalists walk with complaints only when it starts raining. When the rain stops, then the file will be turned off. The same is the case with the roads. When it starts raining, then there is a discussion about the waterlogged road, and when the rain is over, no one has any thoughts or complaints.

From the beginning, the government and the disaster relief forces have been doing rescue work to the best of their ability. the rescue workers moved all the elderly people sick and pregnant were rescued first .. The day before, a woman had said that she had to see the sad view of her old mother and her mentally disabled brother floating away in front of her eyes in the water and she somehow clung to the roof and escaped.

Parvati lost all her courage and thought that her house will also fall over soon. She is waving to all the boats in sight and no one cares. Everyone was trying to search for the trapped anywhere .While she was staying there disappointed, she saw a helicopter hovering over the house, she started waving one end of her sari as high as she could. Although the helicopter left at that time it returned there after an hour. They dropped a rope in front of her. She somehow entered the seat at its end, climbed up and rescued. Even at that time, there was heavy rain. The helicopter brought her to the new headquarters of the camp. There is no place to sit or lie down. What a crowd. What a pitiful sight. There is nothing for the common people to do. There is no shortage of rain and wind till now. Shiva Shiva!, a perversion of nature! When nature took out all its vikadatha, man began to become one. Perhaps it may be mischief that was created to unite people who are divided by different ideas, ambitions, politics, and a sense of nationalism.

Several people were saved when the rescue work was not limited to the government or the disaster relief forces. Those in the floodless areas took the initiative to collect and distribute drinking water, clothes, food, napkins, mats, and blankets. Parvati's children ordered bottled water and napkins to many camps. While the new generation's dress code, conduct, and behavior are questionable for some nowadays, nobody cares about their service attitude. The fact is that many such children were in camps for several days for service . What a good country. Many things were reaching even from nearby places. How many foreign countries have forgotten all disagreements and extended a helping hand? The army traveled by air and delivered food to all the camps. But where ever people are stuck? How many poor people were washed away in the water? no count at all.

Parvati reached the camp by hanging on to the navy helicopter. Bindu, who was fully pregnant, was preparing for her second delivery when the flood came and she also reached the camp by helicopter. From there she was transferred to the hospital under the leadership of the navy. There she gave birth to a beautiful baby girl.

The poor people were brought to the hospitals and given the necessary treatment. for many poor people, it was a good time as they got food and shelter as per usual time.

It was only when she reached the camp that she realized the horror of the flood. Meanwhile, it was interesting to hear that a girl named Rima, who was lying in bed for years in a nearby village, was very surprised to see the water coming in and woke up and ran out of bed. In any case, the flood created a terrible atmosphere in the country. All the small huts were washed away. The poor people were in trouble when it rained. They had no house to go to. Even then, some humanitarians came forward and gave many people a place to build a house and also built some houses. For all this, there were a lot of groups of young people including students, regardless of caste, creed, and color. They helped to clean mud-covered roads and houses along with the army. If anyone see the diligence shown by the children, they will understand the unity in the diversity of the country.

A week later, Parvati went to the house and saw that the house was covered in mud and broken. The Sobha setty chairs on the ground floor were all broken. The rescue workers took it all and put it outside. They saw a cobra under the fridge. Somehow they narrowly escaped from its attack. All the utensils in the kitchen were swept away. The house was a sight to behold. Anyway, as soon as they saw the mud-covered house, she was taken back to the camp. Later, it was cleaned after a week with the intervention of her children.

The low-lying areas took weeks to become habitable. Then for some time, the channel discussion was on the reason for the flood. The level of rain was more than every year. Everyone agrees, but if a certain amount of water was released every day, a flood like this could have been avoided. A politician may not be a diplomat to rule. If such persons are placed in positions of authority,this kind of difficulties may occur. But the silent pain and sighs of those who have lost their dear ones' homes, and shelters will be a curse.

In any case, Parvati despite her ego, in the end needed the hands of a Punjabi to escape. What a great lesson this flood teaches to man. No one can forget that civilian who saved a child when the bridge broke and swept away from his father's hand. ...Although this country is full of different castes, religions, and political ideologies all are united especially in needy situations.

Parvati's children proudly told their mother that their country was praising us for our unity in our diversity .When an emergency came, we faced the disaster together regardless of all our dislikes. The service of the fishermen was immemorable.

After the flood, the schools did not open for a month as most of them were in relief camps as there were still a few people who had no way to go. Those whose houses were fully destroyed. Parvati gave some of them facilities in s home. She also gave a lot of money, dresses, etc. Thus, the great disaster of the flood became a model to show our unity in diversity. It is true to say that there will be good in any misfortune. Parvati's change of behaviour, the sincere service of the fishermen, and the bedridden patient's recovery, the social service of the youth are some silver linings between the flood disasters. Even then, there is nothing to replace the pains of those who have lost their loved ones, homes, and those who have lost their all income sources. When seeing the rain, everyone's prayer is that such a flood will never happen again.

About the Authors

Kajari Guha

Armed with the treasure of decades of experience as an English teacher for the Senior Secondary students of a renowned school of India, Kajari Guha is a published author with great command over English, Bengali and Hindi. She penned several academic books for the students of English who would like to improve English language. Memoirs like Bridging the gap, Don't know Why, Athocho Tumi Udasin, Rangeen, Mahakte Khwab and the stories and poems included in the anthologies like Echoes of Ages Yudh Shastra, The Lyrics and The Character-Sketch with tiny tales,the stories of Pinky Mehra,Born to thrive, the comic con like Pink, Rick and Pip....the Scuba Divers, Euphoric Vendetta-a thriller and many more published by Ukiyoto ,have already garnished the platter of her literary cuisine to captivate even the jaded palates of the readers worldwide. She has translated "Tulsi Ramayana 1008 panktite niboddho" from Hindi to Bengali which has been published from Houston TX,USA.

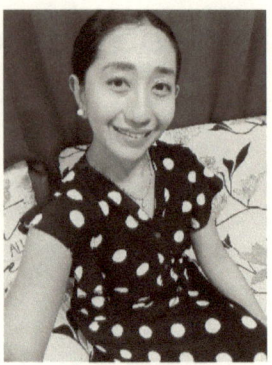

Rhodesia

Rhodesia is a multifaceted individual—a Filipina physician, past professor of Medical Biochemistry, past clinical and academic administrator, author, painter, and poet. At the remarkable age of nine, she was celebrated as the Philippines' Youngest Author for compiling an anthology of poems. While presently dedicated to being a loving mother of two, she continues to contribute to the well-being of others through teleconsultations, all the while reigniting her passion for the written word.

Aurobindo Ghosh

Aurobindo Ghosh a versatile personality After completing B.Sc, M.Sc, M.Phil, Ph.D in Statistics and Ph.D in Economics, Dr. Aurobindo Ghosh taught both under graduate and post graduate students of statistics in Government of Maharashtra College for almost 35 years. After retirement, he joined various Management institutions as Principal across India. His first poetry book "Lily on the northern sky" was published by Notion Press bagged the award from Ukiyoto Publishing, and subsequently translated in French, German, Spanish and Arabic languages. He is a regular contributor of Ukiyoto publisher's anthologies. Side by side he also engaged himself in creating acrylic, Warli and Madhubani paintings. Dr Aurobindo Ghosh writes poems, short stories in different languages specifically in English, Bengali, Hindi, Gujarati and Marathi. His other literary creations are Insight Outsight; a collection of short stories in English, Mejoder golpo, a collection of short stories in Bengali and Chhondo Hole Mondo Ki; a collection of poems in Bengali. His latest solo book, "Bimladadi's dream" is getting published by Ukiyoto Publishing.

Dr. Yogesh A Gupta

Dr. Yogesh A. Gupta is a senior consultant physician who has been practicing for 20 years in Ahmedabad, India. He has written three books and multiple short stories. He aims to present a real-time picture of society in his own words, depicting instances from his life that offer various perspectives. The characters in his stories are inspired by people he has encountered throughout his life.

Moumita De

Moumita De is a prolific author has made significant contribution to the world of literature. She is honoured by various awards for her writings. She explores diverse themes, showcasing a rich literary repertoire.

Dr. Renuka. KP

Mrs. Renuka K.P. a retired Tahsildar is a native of Ernakulam district in Kerala. After her retirement, she spends most of her time as a blogger on social media and has a YouTube channel also. She has published two story books in English and one in Malayalam. She has also written stories in some anthologies and received several recognitions for her literary works. Recently WCEPC has awarded her an Honorary Doctorate in Literature with their membership. Her stories have been translated into four foreign languages.

www.ingramcontent.com/pod-product-compliance
Lightning Source LLC
LaVergne TN
LVHW041543070526
838199LV00046B/1814